WILLIAM
THE
CURIOUS

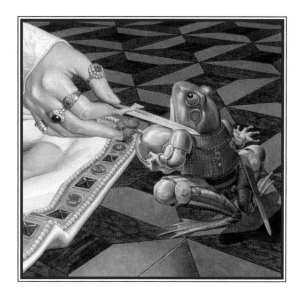

This book is dedicated to all the creatures in the moat.
—C.S.

13-Digit ISBN: 978-1-60433-474-6
10-Digit ISBN: 1-60433-474-6

This book may be ordered by mail from the publisher. Please include $4.99 for postage and handling.
Please support your local bookseller first!

Books published by Cider Mill Press Book Publishers are available at special discounts for bulk purchases in the United States by corporations, institutions, and other organizations. For more information, please contact the publisher.

Applesauce Press is an imprint of
Cider Mill Press Book Publishers
"Where good books are ready for press"
12 Spring Street
PO Box 454
Kennebunkport, Maine 04046

Visit us on the web!
www.cidermillpress.com

Design by Alicia Freile, Tango Media
Typeset in Adobe Caslon Pro
Printed in China

1 2 3 4 5 6 7 8 9 0
First Edition

WILLIAM THE CURIOUS

KNIGHT OF THE WATER LILIES

Written and illustrated by
CHARLES SANTORE

Kennebunkport, Maine

More than a thousand years before you were born, there was a beautiful Queen who lived in a gray stone castle so tall that its walls seemed to touch the clouds and stars. From her windows high in the castle, the Queen could look out in every direction to see the lands she ruled. Her kingdom stretched so far into the distance that she could not see the ends, and it was so wide that she could not see the edges. She called her kingdom the Land of Far and Wide.

But instead of being proud of her beautiful country, the Queen thought it needed improvement, and therefore was always angry and impatient. She would scold her goldsmiths and weavers, and fume at her tapestries, rare ivories, and silks. She was never quite pleased with her ladies-in-waiting, and not quite content with her luxurious throne. She would look out at the hills and trees and grassy pastures and say, "Maybe I should have that mountain moved over just a little more to the left. Yes, that's it!" Or she would say, "That forest is much too green. I want it fixed at once! Get it out of my sight." And finally she would exclaim, "Oh, will I never be happy until the Land of Far and Wide is perfect in every way?"

If the Queen had looked straight down from her windows, she would have seen the moat that encircled the castle to keep enemies away. The moat was covered with beautiful white water lilies that looked like a soft white blanket. But the Queen always looked out at the distant hills and valleys and lakes of the Land of Far and Wide. She never, ever looked down at the moat. If she had, she might have seen William looking up at her as he perched on a lily pad.

William was a small green frog who lived in the moat with his brothers and sisters, and his fishy friends. William wasn't the handsomest frog in the moat, nor the largest, nor the strongest. He was, you might say, a pretty ordinary fellow. Still, there were two things about William that made him different. The first was the little red vest he wore—this came from a toy knight he had found at the bottom of the moat. The second was his curiosity. William was terribly interested in everything that was going on around him. He often sat quietly near the drawbridge, watching and listening, from early morning, when the drawbridge was lowered, until night, when the great clanking chain pulled the drawbridge shut.

The large wooden drawbridge stretched across the moat to the gateway of the castle. Nobody could enter or leave the castle except by crossing the drawbridge, which was guarded by two giant soldiers in shining armor. If enemies approached, the guards could pull the drawbridge up so that no one could cross.

William watched the Queen's knights, with their bright helmets and swords and shields, as they thundered off on horseback to move the distant mountain this way or that, as the Queen demanded. He saw the Queen's sea captains sail away in their mighty ships trying to catch the sun before it sank into the western sea—for the Queen wanted it for her own castle garden.

William was also curious about what was happening inside the castle, and he liked to listen to the conversations of the guards on the drawbridge. That's how he knew that everything inside the castle was very, very beautiful. The Queen never left her home, so she made each of the two hundred rooms as beautiful as could be.

When the Queen's visitors left the castle and crossed over the drawbridge, they would often exclaim, "What a magnificent place!" Inside the castle, William learned, the air was filled with the sweet smells of flowers. In the gardens were rare and beautiful birds, brought from forests beyond the hills. Bright-plumed peacocks paraded along pathways made of rubies and emeralds. Everywhere, magical golden harps played beautiful soft music. Everything the Queen touched and everything she looked upon was almost perfect. But still she was not satisfied. Finally, one day she decided that *almost* perfect was simply not good enough.

The Queen ordered that the royal court and all the servants and guards of the castle should come immediately to her golden throne room.

When everyone was assembled, she announced, "I have decided that everything in the castle must be *absolutely* perfect! You must find each thing that is worn or broken or faded. When you find a cloth with even one broken thread, or a jewel that doesn't glitter enough, or a vase or statue with even the tiniest chip on it, throw it out of the nearest window at once! This is the new castle law."

"Yes, Your Majesty," said the royal court and the servants. And they all began their search.

Meanwhile, outside in the moat, William and his friends sat on their lily pads in the lazy afternoon sun, croaking happy songs. William was beginning to feel rather sleepy. His eyelids were almost closed when there was a loud splash as a copper kettle hit the water from the window above. "Wow! That was close! What's going on?" said William. But nobody knew the answer. Then things began to fall from all the castle windows—down into the waters of the moat.

Splish, splish, splish, splish! Fifty broken buttons made little splashes.

Ker-splash! A cracked cup and some slightly bruised apples and pears landed right next to William.

Kaba-SPLUNGE! A huge oak table—with one tiny scratch—smashed into the water.

By the time night came, the moat was as ugly as a junkyard. The lilies were all gone and the fish were afraid to swim. The sandy bottom was covered with soggy books and rusting armor and swords.

"I just don't understand why anyone would want to destroy our moat," said William sadly. The others listened and nodded in silence.

"Well, maybe it is just a mistake," added William. "Maybe tomorrow the Queen's guards will be sent to clean out the moat. Let's wait and see."

The next morning, William awoke early. The moat was very quiet. The birds did not sing. The fish did not splash and the insects did not buzz. All were still, waiting to see what the day would bring.

Swoosh! Splash! Splattery-splat! The castle guards were throwing things from the windows again. Down came draperies and rugs, sofas and chairs, needles and pins—everything you could imagine.

The same thing happened every day for a whole week. Soon, so much junk filled the moat that the fish and frogs had almost no room left to swim and hop.

"What can we do?" cried William. Nobody answered, because everyone was too busy searching for a safe place to hide.

"I know," William decided. "I will go to the drawbridge to listen. Perhaps I will learn something." With that, he hopped off into the dark, dirty water.

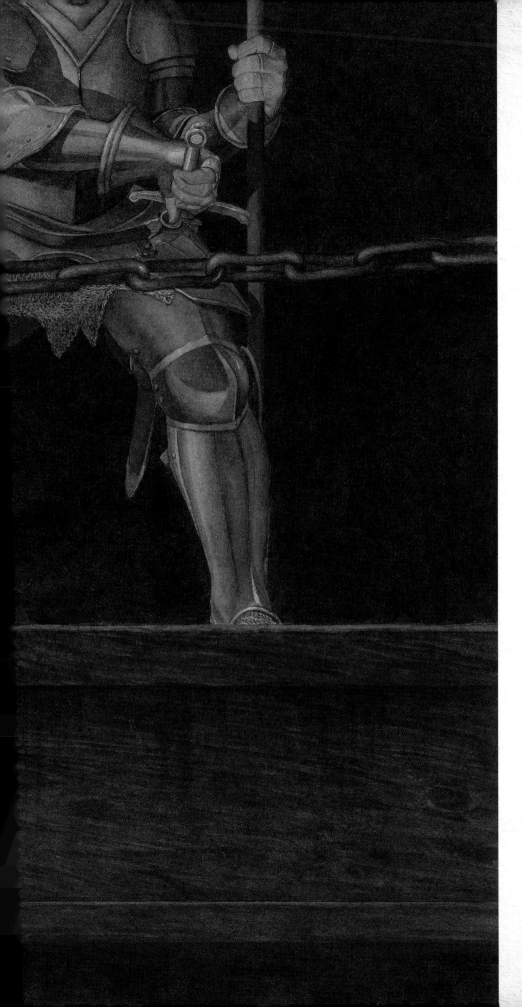

Sure enough, at the drawbridge two of the Queen's giant guards were talking. William listened and became very curious when he heard about the Queen's new law. Why must everything be perfect? William wondered. He just did not understand.

So, when the guards were directly above him, William called out as loudly as he could in his croaky frog voice: "Why is 'perfect' important?"

The guards were startled to hear such a voice breaking through the dark, silent night. They quickly held out torches to light the moat below. "Who is down there?" they shouted. "Friend or foe?"

William moved into the glow of the torches. "I am William," he said, "and I am a friend. I have come to ask why perfect is important."

"Ha, ha ha! Ho, ho!" The guards laughed so hard that their loud voices echoed off the damp stones of the castle. "*You* question the Queen!" one of them bellowed. "A little green frog wants to come up from the moat to ask the Queen 'why.'" "Ha, ha! Ho, ho! Be off, you silly toad," added the other.

Slowly, sadly, William hopped away. All the rest of the night he hopped along the edge of the moat, trying to figure out how to ask the Queen about "perfect," but he shivered when he remembered how large and scary the guards had looked.

By the time the soft rays of dawn began to peek out from behind the hills, William had hopped almost all the way around the huge castle. In the early morning light, William could see clearly how the Queen had destroyed the moat, and he became sadder and more curious than ever. How could *this* be "perfect"? All that was left of the moat's beauty was one lonely water lily.

Just then, he noticed something.

Lying next to the water lily was a little toy knight with a broken foot, tossed out because it was no longer perfect. The knight was dressed like one of the Queen's own brave knights. He had a red vest like William's and a helmet with bright red feathers. In one hand was a small sword, and in the other was a shield. He was buckled up tightly from head to toe in brightly shining armor.

William looked at the toy knight and thought, "If only I could be a knight. Then I could see the Queen and ask her why she has to be perfect and spoil our moat."

William's daydream ended when he heard a loud *bump-thump* coming from the castle. He looked up and saw a huge iron kitchen pot balanced on the window sill above him. Two of the Queen's cooks were holding it. One said, "Must we pour out all of this soup?" "Yes," replied the other. "The Queen tasted it at supper last night and said, 'Too much salt,' and you know what the new law says."

With that, they tilted the pot, and the soup poured down like a waterfall into the moat. Bits of carrots and potatoes floated where the lily pads once had been. All around William, the water was thick and brown and ugly.

William's sadness changed to anger. Just then, the first rays of orange sunlight shone over the edge of the mountains and fell upon the broken toy knight. Slowly, the tiny sword began to glow in a magical way. As the little frog looked at the sword, and then at the water lily, he felt a kind of spell come over him. "I wonder if it fits!" thought William, and he quickly removed the toy knight's helmet and placed it on his own head. He put on the armor and grabbed the toy sword and shield. Then, very gently, he reached for the last water lily left in the moat. He lifted it out of the water and placed it on his shield. Dressed exactly like the toy knight, William hopped as fast as he could to the castle entrance.

At the drawbridge, two mountains of armor with glaring eyes blocked the castle entrance. They were the same two guards who had laughed at him the night before.

William took a deep breath and then raised his shining, magical sword. "Stand aside. I have a gift for the Queen—a rare gift. And I ask only that she answer one question in return," croaked William.

"Ha!" said a guard. "Now the frog dresses himself as a knight! Knights are men, not frogs, you foolish toad!" Then, as fast as lightning, the guard swung his sword at William.

Ssswash! William jumped, but the sharp tip of the blade sliced through his armor and into his arm. William was hurt and frightened, but he stood his ground.

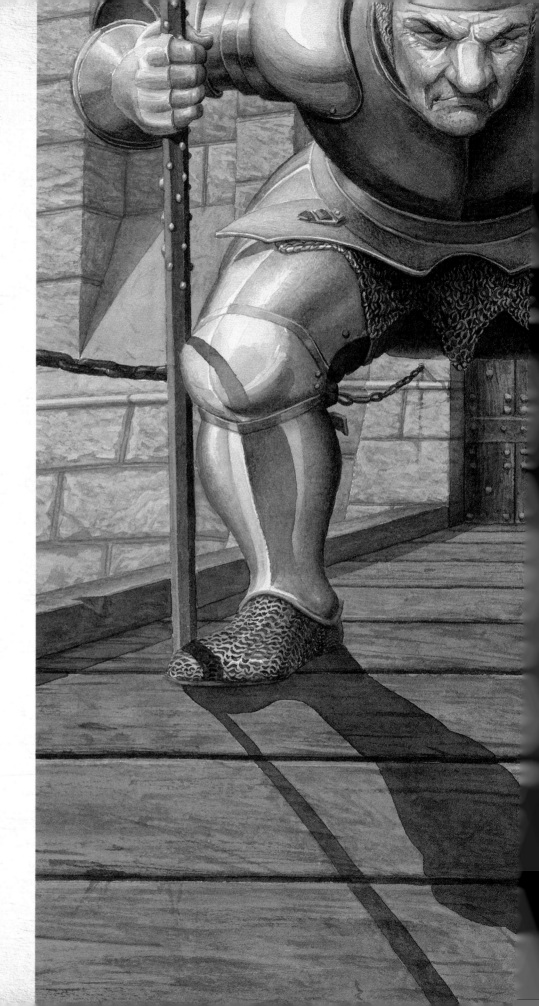

As the guard approached again, William raised his magical sword over his head and charged with all his strength and fury. Again and again the mighty guards flashed their swords at William, and again and again they missed. William hopped left and right, faster and faster. The guards shouted in anger as their weapons smashed into wood and stones, missing little William. *Clank! Clank!*—a dozen times, and then, *flash!* William hopped right onto the guards' feet and *one! two! three!* stuck his little sword through the chain mail into their big, hairy feet.

"Eee-ooww!" screamed the guards. "Ouch! Ouch! *Ouch!*"

High above in the castle, the Queen heard the screaming and clanking of swords and was quite upset. She called one of her servants and said, "Look out my window and tell me what is happening at the drawbridge."

"Your guards are trying to catch a frog, Your Majesty, and the frog—well, the frog is dressed like a knight!" the servant replied.

"Ridiculous!" said the Queen. "Bring all three of them to me at once."

Soon William and the two guards appeared at the door of the Queen's beautiful throne room. William gazed about in wonder. "Come to me at once," commanded the Queen.

Courteously, William took off his helmet as he entered the golden room. He hopped proudly, paying no attention to the wound on his arm. The guards hobbled forward. Their feet hurt so much that they could barely walk.

"What's the matter with you two? Walk tall and straight, like proper guards of the drawbridge!" ordered the Queen.

"We are sorry, Your Majesty—but this nasty frog has cut up our feet," said one guard.

"Your Majesty should be careful," said the other. "This frog is dangerous. He says he has a gift for Your Majesty, and all he asks is an answer to one question. But he *cannot* be trusted."

"Stop your whimpering! I am ashamed of you. Guards who cannot even catch a small frog! Go back to the drawbridge. This little fellow seems harmless enough—I will talk with him," said the Queen. The guards limped away.

After the door closed, the Queen turned angrily to William. "Now, tell me your name," she said. Still frightened, William began slowly in a soft, croaking voice: "I am William, Your Majesty, your loyal subject, and I live in the castle moat. Our moat was very lovely and I have brought you its rarest treasure. All I ask in return is your answer to a question. Just one question, Your Majesty." With that, William bowed deeply and placed the water lily at her feet.

The Queen looked at it closely and said, "Oh, what a beautiful and perfect flower! But surely not a rare treasure. Is the moat not covered with such flowers? Bring me more tomorrow—without so much fuss." Then she frowned and added impatiently, "I thank you for your gift, but I still cannot imagine what question could be so important that you would attack my guards!"

William spoke again. "Your Majesty, if you would come to the window, you shall see that this is truly a rare and special flower."

"Very well," the Queen answered. "I shall show you my beautiful new hill covered with lavender."

William hopped to the window ledge as the Queen pointed into the distance. "Now, isn't that just *perfect?*" she said.

"Yes, Your Majesty, the hills and mountains are a lovely sight. But may I ask you to move closer to the window and look straight down?" For the first time, the Queen looked down at the moat, far, far below. "Oh, how ugly and awful!" she shrieked, putting her hands to her cheeks as she stared at the junk pile that the moat had become. There were no flowers. The water was dark, and green slime covered the surface.

William gathered up his courage and at last was able to ask his question. "Your Majesty," he said quietly. "This lily was the very last flower left in the moat. Here in your beautiful castle, perhaps there is some pool or pond where it could live and blossom. Your Majesty, why is 'perfect' so important?"

"Is that your question, William? I will tell you, but first I must know who is responsible for this horrible mess!" she cried.

Almost as soon as she had said this, the Queen realized exactly what had caused all the ugliness below and how perfectly thoughtless she had been. There were tears in her eyes as she looked down at the moat.

She turned once again to her tiny visitor. "Perhaps 'perfect' is not so important after all. In my quest to be perfect, both in my castle and far and wide, I have forgotten to care for the things under my very own window."

The Queen thought carefully for a few moments and then asked, "So the moat was once a wonderful place to live for you and your family and friends?"

"Yes," replied William. "I came here hoping that Your Majesty would stop being 'perfect,' so the moat could be beautiful again."

Again the Queen paused in thought—and her brow slowly began to unwrinkle. "You are brave, William. You may tell everyone that it shall be done!" she exclaimed.

At that, William smiled and bowed deeply. His wound was beginning to ache and he felt dizzy, but he was very, very happy. As he turned to leave, the Queen's face lit up, as if she had thought of an idea even more wonderful than perfection. With a twinkle in her eye, she said, "Sir William, may I borrow your sword?"

"Oh, I am not a knight, Your Majesty," said William as he gave the Queen his tiny magical sword. "I took this armor from a broken toy knight I found in the castle moat. I am just a frog."

"Now you are a knight," the Queen said, kneeling and touching his shoulder gently with the sword. "I name you Sir William, Knight of the Water Lilies, Protector of the Castle Moat."

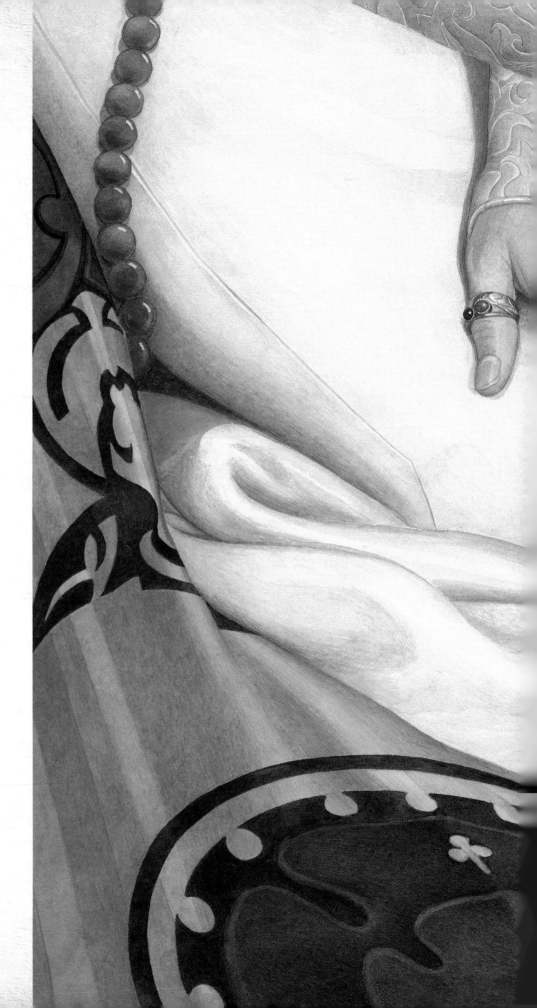

The Queen kept her word. Soon, with Sir William's help, being "perfect" was no longer as important to her, and after a time the moat was as beautiful as before. The frogs and fish and turtles and dragonflies and mayflies and all the other creatures lived happily once again.

Now, more than a thousand years later, the castle is still standing. If you visited there tomorrow and walked onto the drawbridge, you would see a soft blanket of white water lilies floating on the moat's surface. If you looked closely, you would also see one curious lily—not a perfect lily at all, but red like the feather in the helmet of a tiny knight.

And if you watched carefully, the beautiful flower might unfold its fiery petals and remind you of a very special fellow: Sir William the Curious, the brave little frog whose gift to the Queen saved his home, and who became known forever as Knight of the Water Lilies, Protector of the Castle Moat.

KNIGHT OF THE WATER LILIES